The Boy Who Loved Horses

Original title: Big Horse, Little Horse

By MARTHA GOLDBERG

Pictures by JOE LASKER

SCHOLASTIC BOOK SERVICES
NEW YORK · TORONTO · LONDON · AUCKLAND · SYDNEY · TOKYO

. for Ethel

This book is sold subject to the condition that it shall not be resold, lent, or otherwise circulated in any binding or cover other than that in which it is published—unless prior written permission has been obtained from the publisher—and without a similar condition, including this condition, being imposed on the subsequent purchaser.

This edition has been especially edited for Lucky Book Club Readers.

Text copyright © 1960 by Martha Goldberg. Illustrations copyright © 1963 by Scholastic Magazines, Inc. This edition is published by Scholastic Book Services, a division of Scholastic Magazines, Inc., by arrangement with Macmillan Publishing Co., Inc., publishers of the book under the title BIG HORSE, LITTLE HORSE.

10th printing .... January 1975

Printed in the U.S.A.

This story is about a Mexican boy named Mateo. You know, of course, that in Mexico everyone speaks Spanish. Here are some Spanish words you will find in this book:

Si means *yes*.

Si, Señor means *yes, sir*.

Adios means *good-by*.

Plaza is an open place in the center of the village.

Tortillas are Mexican bread. They look like pancakes.

Olla is a large jar. It is used to carry water.

Burro is a donkey.

Mateo's family are potters. They make pots and toys out of clay. Here are some words that have to do with making pottery:

A **kiln** is a small oven for baking clay pottery. The pottery is not ready until it is baked.

To **fire** a pot means to bake it in a kiln.

Early one morning, Mateo led his burro down the mountain. The little burro was almost buried under a heavy load of firewood. It stopped to rest on the trail.

"Get up, slow one. Mama is waiting for the wood," Mateo said. He tapped the burro lightly with a stick.

Far below were the red tile roofs of Mateo's village. There each family made the black pottery which was famous all over Mexico.

Mateo's mother was one of the finest potters of the village. Today she would fire the *ollas* — the large water jars. So Mateo hurried with the wood.

For still another reason he hurried. He wanted to see the beautiful brown horse, Panchita, who belonged to Big Pablo.

On his way from the mountain he had often stopped to watch her. He had even tried to model a clay horse. But his horses had never looked like Panchita. Mateo wanted to see her again before he tried to make another clay horse.

Mateo was sure that he could make a good clay horse. This was a secret that no one knew.

quickly. Near Big Pablo's home, the horse Panchita was out in the field. She ran in wide, joyful circles. She rolled over and rubbed her back on the ground. She kicked her heels in the air like a colt. Mateo laughed to see her.

Now he could see why his little clay horse had not looked like Panchita. He had given it long ears like a *burrito!* Panchita's ears were small. Her mane and tail were long and silky. "When I get home," Mateo thought, "I will know how to make a clay horse that looks like her."

Big Pablo came to him as he stood watching Panchita.

"Good day, *Señor*," Mateo called out.

"Good day, Mateo," Big Pablo answered. "Look well at Panchita, for soon she will be gone. I will take her to the Saturday Market."

Mateo was shocked. "You will sell Panchita!" he said. "What a pity."

How could anyone want to sell so fine a horse? "Panchita is worth many *burritos*," he said to Big Pablo. "She is big and strong, and she runs very fast."

"That is true," Big Pablo answered. "But also Panchita eats much. I must sell her. May the Almighty One grant her a good home."

Mateo turned away. He was too sad to speak. He drove the burro slowly along the road. If Panchita left the village, he would never see her again. She must not leave!

Then Mateo had an idea. His family could use a horse. He would ask his father to buy her.

When Mateo reached home, his father called out, "Mama is waiting for the wood. Where have you been so long?"

"I stopped at Big Pablo's," Mateo answered.

"You stopped while we waited for you?" his father asked.

"*Si*," Mateo said, all in a rush. "Big Pablo is selling Panchita. Please, Papa, can we not buy her?"

"Do you know why Big Pablo sells her, little son?" his father asked.

"*Si*, Papa," Mateo said.

"Are we so rich, then, that I should buy a

horse? Should I buy a horse because my son has set his heart on it? A horse, ha! Next you will be asking that I buy a motorcar. Go and unload the wood, foolish one. Let me hear no more about Panchita."

Mateo said nothing. He led the burro to the woodpile. Quickly he took the wood off the burro's back and put it on the woodpile. Then he took the burro to his father. His father was going back to the mountain for some more firewood.

After his father left, Mateo went into the house for a lump of the grayish-brown clay. He came back to the woodpile and sat down on the ground behind it. Now no one would see him.

Mateo began to work quickly with the clay. First he rolled it into a ball. Then he wet his fingers in a bowl of muddy water and smoothed the ball of clay. He pinched one end to make the head and the tiny ears. Then he made the legs and tail out of the small rolls of clay.

He held up the little horse to look at it. It was not right. A horse was harder to make than a clay whistle in the shape of a bird. A horse was harder to make than an angel whose wide skirt was really a bell. These things his mother had taught him to make. But he knew he could make his horse now. Would he have time to make it before someone found his hiding place?

He bent the soft clay legs. Now his little horse began to look like the big horse Panchita running across the field. As he worked, he thought of the answers he might have given his father: A horse would make quick work of plowing the cornfield. A horse could carry the pottery to market in large bags hung over her sides. He and Concha and Baby Rosita could all ride on her, too. Could a burro carry so much?

But there was one big question he could not answer: What would they feed Panchita?

"Mateo! Mateo!" It was his sister Concha calling him.

Mateo pushed himself still closer to the house.

Concha soon grew tired of looking for him. Her voice faded away. Now all was quiet as Mateo worked. He drew with his fingernail to make the horse's mane. He used a tiny stick to mark the eyes and nose. Then with wet fingers he smoothed over the little clay body again.

"Mateo! You are there! Come here!"

It was Mama calling him this time. She was angry.

Mateo knew he must answer her. He covered the clay horse with his hand. Then he walked into the *patio*.

"I am here, *Mamacita*," he said.

"Why did you not come when I sent Concha for you?" his mother asked.

Mateo held out the horse for her to see. "I was making this," he said. "I wanted to finish it."

Mama took the little horse gently into her hands.

"It is good," she said in a surprised voice.

"May I fire it?" Mateo asked eagerly.

"If you wish," Mama said, "but it is very small and thin. It may break in the firing."

"Then I shall make a larger one," Mateo said quickly.

"No, my son," his mother shook her head. "You must make the toys that we can sell. No one buys clay horses."

Mateo turned his head away to hide the tears in his eyes. Not to make a little horse like Panchita! Soon she would be gone forever. It was almost too much to bear.

His mother did not seem to notice how Mateo felt. She went on talking "Mateo, your grandmother has a fever. I must take food to her. There is work for you to do while I am gone."

"Do you wish me to watch the fire?"

"I could not fire the water jars this morning," his mother said. "You came too late with the wood."

"I watched Panchita for a little while," Mateo explained.

"Always you watch Panchita," his mother said. "Will you never learn to come when we are waiting for you?"

Mateo hung his head and said in a low voice, "I am ashamed, Mama."

"Do not do it again, little son," his mother said. She went quickly into the house and brought out a large basket. She placed the basket on a table against the *patio* wall.

Then Mateo's mother saw his sad face. She put her hand on Mateo's shoulder and said with a smile, "It is well that there is no fire to watch. I must go away today."

"I will go with you to grandmother's house," Mateo said.

"No, son," his mother said. "Rafael is bringing the tourists to see how the black pottery is made. You and Concha must be ready. You must help me."

Mama and Papa had good reason to be angry with him this morning, Mateo thought. But he would show them that he could do his work well. Then maybe Mama would let him make a clay horse some other day.

"Concha and I will do as you wish, *Mamacita*," he said. "When will you return?"

"By the next bus," his mother said. She moved quickly as she spoke.

Mateo went after her, watching as she took *tortillas*, beans, and chicken for grandmother and placed them in the basket. She covered the food with a clean cloth.

Then she said, "You must sweep the *patio* and set out the chairs. Also, you must have the clay ready. Cover it well with a wet cloth."

Mateo nodded.

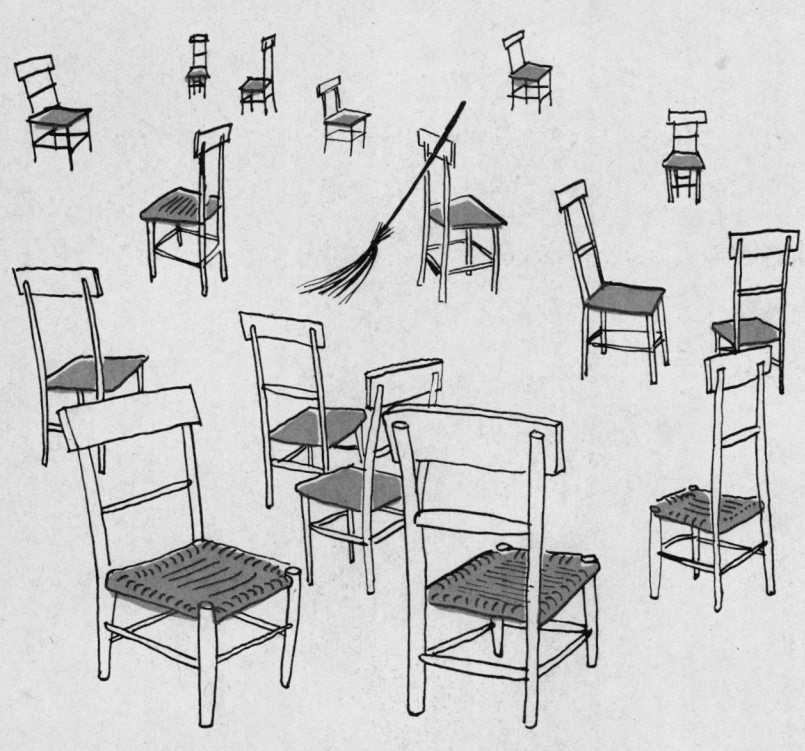

"Put out a large *olla* — one that is almost dry. I will decorate it as the tourists watch," his mother added. "And on the big table put the toys and bowls we have made to sell."

"*Si*," Mateo said. "Concha and I will polish them well."

"Take care that you do all that I have told you to do," his mother said.

"Do not worry, *Mamacita*," Mateo answered.

Just then Concha ran into the yard. She called, "*Mamacita! Mamacita!* The bus! The bus is coming."

"I will go now," Mama said.

She tied Baby Rosita tightly in her shawl. Then she placed a roll of cloth like a crown on the top of her head. On this she set the basket of food.

"*Adios!* Till we meet again," she said as she started down the road.

"*Adios, Mamacita!*" Mateo and Concha answered. "Go with God."

Turning around, Mama called back, "Mateo, if it rains you must carry in the firewood and the jars that are drying in the sun."

"I will remember," Mateo called after her.

Concha took a broom and began to sweep the *patio*. Mateo wet the ground to settle the dust.

Next, he and Concha carried the chairs into the patio. They put them in a circle. Each chair faced the mat where Mama would sit later to work the clay.

They cleaned off the big table and brought out the basket of small toys. They polished the toys with a soft cloth until the whistles and bells and little dishes made of black pottery shone in the bright sunshine.

Mama would be pleased.

"Concha," Mateo said, "go to the *plaza* and wait for the bus. Carry the baby so that Mama may come quickly."

After Concha had gone, Mateo squatted on the ground. How his fingers wanted to make another clay horse — a clay horse that would

remind him of Panchita. If only Mama would let him make such a horse!

As he waited, a few drops of rain fell. Then all at once the rain poured down. It was like a solid wall of water.

Mateo jumped up. He must carry in the firewood. It should be dry when Mama made a fire in the kiln. He would get the *ollas* later.

He ran to the woodpile and picked up an armload of branches. He held them against his body. They tickled and scratched him as he ran. Mateo dropped the branches on the dry ground under the roof of the open shed. Then he ran back for more.

He came to the opening in the cactus fence and went quickly out to the road. "Concha! Concha!" he called. But he did not wait to see if she would come.

Mateo ran back to the woodpile. He filled his arms with branches again. His clothes dripped with water. His bare feet were covered with mud. Back and forth he ran.

The rain poured down, making puddles in the yard. Mateo saw that the clay *ollas* were standing in water. Should he stop and put them away before they were spoiled? But what good were clay jars without dry firewood?

"Concha! Concha!" he shouted again in his loudest voice. But he was afraid she would not hear him above the noise of the rain.

Only one armload of wood was left. As Mateo turned to get it, Concha ran in from the road.

Breathless, she picked up two of the large jars. She turned each one over and shook the water from it. She ran with the jars to the house and set them down on the dirt floor.

Mateo went to help her. She was ahead of him. He picked up two jars. Racing after her, he called, "Who will get there first?"

Mateo did not see the little pig that was running across the yard. He tripped over the

pig and fell down. The jars broke into pieces. The pig ran away squealing. Mateo was left on the ground with broken pottery all around him.

Concha was laughing. Mateo got up. He brushed the mud and bits of broken pottery from his hands and clothes. His face was very sad. Again he had done something wrong!

"They were fine big *ollas*," he said sadly. "And I cannot make others for Mama. She will be angry with me."

"But I will tell Mama that the little pig tripped you," Concha told him.

She helped Mateo carry all the big jars into the house. Then Concha and Mateo stood in the open doorway and watched the rain. After a little while, Mateo went out into the yard again to see if they had forgotten anything.

Every stick of firewood and all the *ollas* were under cover. He let out his breath in relief.

Mateo walked back to Concha and said, "You came from the *plaza* just in time."

The *plaza!* The bus! In his hurry Mateo had forgotten it.

"Did not the bus come?" he asked.

Concha shook her head. "They say it has stopped on the bridge."

"The tourists will come soon," Mateo said, "and Mama is not here."

"*Mamacita* will walk," Concha said.

"*Si,*" answered Mateo, "but the tourists in cars will come first."

The rain stopped just as quickly as it had started. The sun shone again in a bright blue sky. The chairs were drying. The water was soaking into the ground.

Concha and Mateo heard the sound of cars in the road. They heard car doors slamming. They heard people talking. The tourists were here! Rafael, the guide, led the tourists into the *patio.*

Mateo ran to Rafael and drew him aside. "All is ready," he whispered, "but Mama is not here. This morning she went to see my grandmother, and she has not come back."

"Do not worry," Rafael said. "I shall show the kiln and the clay. I will also show the clay things your mother has made. She will come soon."

Mateo felt better then. He turned to Concha and said, "Go back to the *plaza* and wait for Mama."

Concha left the *patio* quickly.

The tourists were looking at the small toys on the table. Mateo stood near them. He did not understand their words. But he could tell that they liked the fine toys. He was proud. He and Concha had made these toys. If the little clay horse were here on the table, would the tourists like it too, Mateo wondered.

Rafael called everyone together in the *patio*. He told them how Papa had dug the clay from the bank of the river and cleaned out all the sand and rocks. He told how Mama and Papa wet the dry clay and worked it with their hands until it was soft and ready to use.

Then Rafael took the tourists into the house and showed them the *ollas* — the water jars. He pointed out the other clay things — the cooking pots and baking dishes and the bowls.

"Now," Rafael said, "we will go into the yard and see the kiln where the pottery is fired. Only the potters of this village know the secret of making black pottery."

Papa had dug a deep hole in the ground to make the kiln. Near the bottom he had made a row of bricks. Rafael showed the tourists how Mama put the clay pieces on the row of bricks. He showed them how she covered the clay with bits of broken pottery. He showed them the place underneath the bricks where Mama made the fire. He told them how Mama closed the kiln with earth.

Now it was time for Mama to sit on the straw mat to make an olla. This was the most important part of the visit. But Mama was not here! The tourists had gone back into the *patio*. They were sitting in the chairs. What should Mateo and Rafael do?

Mateo ran to the fence and looked down the road. There he saw people still waiting for the bus. But the bus was on the bridge and would not move.

If Papa were here, he would take Mama's place on the mat and make an *olla*. But it was

many hours before Papa would come back from the mountains. Mama had asked *him, Mateo*, to help with the tourists. He must do what he could.

Mateo walked back into the patio and said to Rafael in a low voice, "I can decorate an *olla*. Perhaps Mama will come while I work on the *olla*."

Rafael spoke to the people seated in the chairs. "Today, Mateo will decorate an *olla*. He is only eight years old, but he is already a good potter."

Mateo had brought a large *olla* from the house. It had been drying for several days, but had not been fired. With a sharp, thin piece of stone, he made fine lines around the neck of the jar. Then, on the widest part of the jar, he drew a large flower with a stem and leaves.

He held the *olla* up to show what he had done. Then he turned the stone over and used the smooth, flat side to polish the jar. He

stopped and held it up again. It was beautiful. He set it down, for it was ready to be fired.

Mateo had worked as long as he could. He had hoped that Mama would come. Now he was finished, and she was not here.

Some of the tourists stood up and began to move about the *patio*. Soon they would go away. They would not see how the black pottery was made.

If only Mama would come, Mateo thought.

He stood up and ran quickly out to the road again. Down near the *plaza* someone was walking. But Mateo could see that it was not Mama. It was a man with a horse. It was Big Pablo taking Panchita away from the village!

A tear ran down Mateo's cheek. "*Adios*, Panchita," he said softly. "Go with God."

Everything has gone wrong today, Mateo thought. He turned and walked slowly back toward the *patio*. Panchita was on her way to market. The tourists were leaving. He had not been able to show them how Mama made the black pottery.

He reached the patio. The tourists were still there. If only he could make an *olla!* But Mama had said that he was too small to work with the large jars. And if he made a little toy whistle or a bell, no one would be able to see.

But he could make a horse like the beautiful Panchita! Today Mama had said that his little horse was good. Should he make a bigger one while the people watched?

He had done so many things wrong today. Mama had told him not to make a bigger horse, but it was the only thing he could do. When Mama came back, he would explain. Only sometimes she did not listen, but punished quickly, he thought.

Mateo sat down on the mat and picked up a ball of the wet clay. Quickly he shaped the round body, the small head, and the tiny ears.

The people began to watch him work. Those who had been standing sat down.

He made the neck with the mane flying in the wind. He formed the legs with rolls of clay. He made the tail with another roll. How like Panchita the little horse was beginning to look!

Mateo held up his work and smiled. The people smiled back. And then Mateo saw his mother. She stood behind the row of chairs with Rafael and Concha. She had been watching as he worked with the clay!

Mateo's fingers grew stiff. The little horse was again just a lump of cold, wet clay in his hands. He wanted to drop it and run away. His

mother was a fine potter. Some said she was the finest potter in all of Mexico. He could not work as she watched. It was *she* who should be here on the mat — not Mateo.

Mateo put the horse down. He waited for his mother to come and take his place. She shook her head. Mateo thought that she did not understand. He stood up and walked toward her. But she shook her head again and pointed to the mat.

Mateo went back to the mat and sat down. Slowly he picked up the little clay horse. Mama wanted him to finish! He could hardly believe it. But she was smiling and waiting for him to go on.

He picked up a sharp stick and drew the eyes. His fingernail made the fine lines on the mane and tail to look like hair. Mateo wet his fingers in the bowl of water and smoothed over the little body. He was finished.

He looked up at his mother.

She came to him, and Mateo said quickly, "I could not make an *olla* like yours, *Mamacita*. I made the big horse like Panchita because I could make nothing else."

"You did well, Mateo," his mother answered. She took the clay horse from him. She turned it over carefully. "It is well made, little son," she said. "It will fire well."

Those were the finest words Mama could say. Mateo was filled with happiness.

The people had left their chairs and were talking to Rafael.

"Many of the tourists would like to buy the horse when it is fired," Rafael said to Mateo. "Will you make others?"